Oliver Moon
and the Nipperbat Nightmare

Sue Mongredien

Illustrated by
Jan McCafferty

USBORNE

For Jamie Tilley, with lots of love

First published in 2007 by Usborne Publishing Ltd., Usborne House,
83-85 Saffron Hill, London EC1N 8RT, England. www.usborne.com

Text copyright © Sue Mongredien, 2007

Illustrations copyright © Usborne Publishing Ltd, 2007

A CIP catalogue record for this book is available from
the British Library.

UK ISBN 9780746077917 First published in America in 2011 AE.

American ISBN 9780794530372 JFMAMJJAS ND/10 01311/1

Printed in Yeovil, Somerset, UK.

Contents

Chapter One

It was the last day of classes at Magic School before the week long Halloween break, and Oliver Moon was in a very good mood. He couldn't wait for school to finish and the fun to start!

"Before you all get your broomsticks and leave, I have a few things to talk to you about," said Mr. Goosepimple,

Oliver's teacher, to the class. "First, some sad news. Hoo-Hoo the owl has announced his retirement. After seven years with us, he's leaving Magic School to go and live in an old owls' nest by the sea, and spend more time with his grandowlets."

"Ahhhh," Hattie Toadtrumper and some of the other girls chorused.

Oliver felt a little sad at the news, too. Hoo-Hoo was the school's Wizardball team mascot, and he was known throughout Cacklewick for his rousing cheers of "Who-Who's the best team? We're the best team!"

"Second, our headmistress, Mrs. MacLizard, has asked me to let you know that..." Mr. Goosepimple's voice trailed away.

"What was it again?" he muttered, scratching his head.

A squeaky little voice piped up from the corner of the room. "Halloween presents!"

Mr. Goosepimple turned gratefully to the cage where Nippy the nipperbat, the class pet, was hanging upside down.

"Thanks, Nippy," Mr. Goosepimple

smiled. "What would I do without you? Yes – that's right. Mrs. MacLizard wanted me to remind you that your Halloween presents should be delivered by her magic messenger spell any time…um…now."

As he finished speaking, an avalanche of orange and black packages rained down in the classroom. It was the school tradition that every year at Halloween, on the last morning of classes, each student put a small wrapped gift into a giant pumpkin in the assembly hall. The gifts were then magically shuffled and given out at random just before it was time to go home.

A small present bounced off Oliver's head and onto his desk. It was wrapped

in orange paper and tied with a black
bow. He opened it quickly to find a silver
box with wisps of blue smoke floating out
of it. *Wish In A Box*, it said, in curly blue
writing on the front. Excellent!

A wish would definitely come in handy.
Oliver was already imagining some
really cool things he could wish for...
A pet scorpion, perhaps, or a bedroom-
cleaning genie, or a neverending supply
of yummy roast cockroaches... "What
did you get?" he asked, turning to his
best friend, Jake Frogfreckle.

Jake's present had landed with a
squelching sound, and was now croaking
loudly from inside its shiny orange paper.
Jake pulled the wrapping off to reveal a
warty brown toad.
The toad belched
grumpily and
stared at
Jake with
yellow eyes.

"Hello, mate," Jake said, tickling it under the chin with his wand.

"Before you leave, there's one last thing," Mr. Goosepimple said. "I need someone to take care of Nippy during the Halloween break. I'd take him myself only…" He had a faraway look in his eyes. "Only, I can't."

"Romantic getaway with Mrs. Goosepimple," Nippy piped up knowingly. "No pets allowed!"

Mr. Goosepimple blushed and ignored Nippy's remark. "So…any volunteers?"

Oliver put up his hand at once. He really liked Nippy, the cute little nipperbat, with his paper-thin black wings and dark, beady eyes. He was always so helpful in class, reciting potion

14

recipes if the students were struggling, or singing funny songs to make them laugh. "I will, sir!" he called out eagerly.

A few of the other young witches and wizards had their hands up, too. Pippi Prowlcat was shouting, "Me, sir! Me, sir!" Colin Cockroach and Lucy Lizardlegs both looked eager, as well. Mr. Goosepimple scratched his beard. "I'll send a magic message to your parents to check if they're happy to look after Nippy," he said, waving his wand. "And whoever replies first can take him."

The class waited for a few moments, and then the blackboard shimmered with a strange violet light.

"Here comes our first reply," said Mr. Goosepimple, gazing at it.

An image of Mrs. Prowlcat appeared on the blackboard, as if it were a television screen. "Definitely not!" she said, folding her arms across her chest and glaring. "I'm allergic, Pippi – and you know that!"

"Oh, please, Mom, come on!" Pippi wheedled, but the image of her mom was already turning fuzzy and fading away.

The blackboard shimmered a fiery red next, and then Mr. and Mrs. Cockroach appeared on it. Mr. Cockroach had a large python around his shoulders and Mrs. Cockroach was cuddling a slit-eyed black cat. "Ooh, we love pets," Mrs. Cockroach said. "The more the merrier in our house, eh, puss-kins?"

The cat stared around the classroom,
its ears pricked up. Then it looked over in
Nippy's direction and licked its lips.
"Meoooow!" it warbled, straining to get
out of Mrs. Cockroach's arms.

"Meeoooww!"

"No way!" Nippy squeaked, hiding behind his wings. "Not them!"

The Cockroaches turned fuzzy and

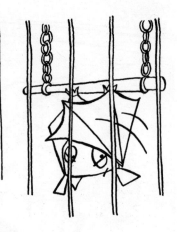

disappeared. "Whew," said Nippy, uncovering his head. "*Anyone* would be better than them."

The blackboard rippled all the colors of the rainbow.

"Come *on,* Mom!" Oliver muttered under his breath. Why was she taking so long to reply to the message?

Then, with a silvery shimmer, a picture of Mrs. Moon, Oliver's mom, appeared on the blackboard. She was bouncing the

Witch Baby, Oliver's sister, on her hip and looking flustered. The Witch Baby had two new fangs coming through, and she was bawling loudly.

"What?" Oliver's mom shouted over the din. "What was that? A nipperbat? Fine. Whatever!"

"YES!" Oliver cheered. "Thanks, Mom!"

Mrs. Moon was nodding and shushing the Witch Baby. "Is that all? Because I must get going," she said distractedly. "All right, my little bogey-lump, sssshhh."

Mr. Goosepimple waved his wand, and the image of Mrs. Moon and the Witch Baby turned fuzzy and vanished. He beamed at Oliver. "Then that's settled," he said.

"But sir—" Lucy moaned.

Mr. Goosepimple shrugged. "Your parents must have been too busy to reply," he said. "Better luck next time."

The clock on the wall suddenly opened its eyes and gave a shrill squeal.

"End of school! End of school!" it cried.

A cheer went up all over Magic School. The Halloween vacation had begun!

Chapter
Two

There was a flurry of excitement as everyone charged to get their cloaks and broomsticks. Jake waited with Oliver while Mr. Goosepimple carried Nippy's cage over. "Now," Mr. Goosepimple said, putting it down carefully, "the most important thing to remember when you're caring for a nipperbat is that they don't like open spaces. They like confined areas — which is why we keep Nippy in a cage. He prefers it that way."

"It's true," Nippy agreed, folding his wings around himself.

"So keep him safely in his cage, and feed him twice a day," Mr. Goosepimple went on. He scooped up some bat food and put it in a brown paper bag. "This is his favorite: powdered jellyfish mixed with chopped phoenix feathers. He likes a few fresh slugs from the garden, too, and pond water to drink. That's it! Easy as pumpkin pie."

"Thanks, sir," Oliver said, smiling shyly at Nippy. "I'm sure you'll have a nice time at our house, Nippy."

Mr. Goosepimple tapped his wand on the cage. "Sha-boom, ding-dong, cage be gone!" he called out loudly. There was a large, black puff of smoke, and then Nippy's cage vanished.

Mr. Goosepimple smiled. "He'll be waiting at home for you," he said. "So hurry back there, won't you?"

"Yes, sir, thank you, sir," Oliver said, stuffing the bat food into his pocket. "Come on, Jake. Let's go!"

Oliver and Jake both lived near enough Magic School to be able to walk there and back every day. Today, though, Oliver couldn't help breaking into a run. He was really excited at the thought of having a nipperbat for a week. It was going to be so much fun!

"You're so lucky, Oliver," Jake said, as they raced along the street. "I'd love to be able to look after Nippy, but my sister has a real thing about bats."

"What, she's scared of them?" Oliver asked in surprise. Jake's sister Mildred was rather fierce, in Oliver's opinion. He couldn't imagine her being scared of anything.

Jake shook his head. "No – she loves *eating* them. Raw. If Nippy was in our house, he wouldn't last two minutes," he replied.

Oliver shuddered at the thought of the clever little nipperbat being gobbled up by Mildred's great jaws. A worried croak came out of Jake's pocket and the toad popped his head out questioningly.

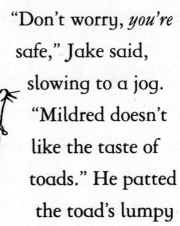

"Don't worry, *you're* safe," Jake said, slowing to a jog. "Mildred doesn't like the taste of toads." He patted the toad's lumpy head. "She might just want to cuddle you, though," he warned. "That's almost as bad, I'm afraid."

They'd reached Oliver's house now. "I'd better go straight home," Jake said reluctantly. "Mom wants me to help her start making the Halloween soup. Bye, Oliver."

"Bye," Oliver replied, running up the path. He pushed open the front door to hear the Witch Baby still wailing from somewhere in the house. Without even going to say hello to his mom, he raced up to his bedroom and opened the door. On the floor by Oliver's spiderweb hammock sat Nippy's cage. And there inside it, sleeping soundly as he hung upside down, was Nippy.

"Oliver, is that you?" came the sound of Mrs. Moon's voice.

Oliver tiptoed out of his room, not wanting to disturb the slumbering creature. "Coming," he called. He went down to the kitchen where Mrs. Moon was dabbing a smelly yellow ointment on the Witch Baby's gums. The Witch Baby was thrashing her arms around and screaming in rage.

"There," sighed Mrs. Moon, wiping her finger on her cloak. "That should do it."

A yellow froth started bubbling out of the Witch Baby's mouth, and she stopped crying immediately. A stream of small bubbles floated into the air and she stared at them with wet eyes, as they hovered in front of her. "Bubble," she said wonderingly, poking at one with a pudgy finger. "Bubble!"

Mrs. Moon plopped the Witch Baby down on the floor.

"What was that your teacher summoned me about?" she asked Oliver wearily. "I could hardly hear what was going on, what with Madam screaming her head off. Something about you doing a nipperbat project at school? Or was it a trip to go and see the nipperbats in Cacklewick Zoo?" A guilty look passed over her face. "I just said yes because I couldn't really think straight."

"Oh," Oliver replied. "Well, it was about taking care of the school nipperbat, Nippy, over Halloween. He's ever so nice, Mom, and—"

"Ooh, no, I don't think so," Mrs. Moon said, shaking her head. "Not with your sister. She's not very gentle with small creatures, is she?"

Oliver crossed his fingers quickly. "The thing is, Mom," he replied, "you already said yes, didn't you? So Nippy's here. In my bedroom."

Mrs. Moon stared at Oliver. "In your bedroom?" she echoed.

Oliver nodded. "Is that all right? Only…"

"I suppose it'll have to be," Mrs. Moon sighed and she glanced up at the calendar. "He *is* good, isn't he? Only we've got the Wartwhistles coming over for dinner on Halloween night, and you know how snooty they are. I don't want anything to go wrong." She looked down at the Witch Baby. "You'll have to keep Nippy away from your sister, too."

"No problem," Oliver said. "And he's really good," he added. "Promise. You'll hardly know he's there. He's a very nice nipperbat."

The Witch Baby looked up, with a

bubble on her head. "Nipperbat?" she repeated, sounding interested. "Nice. Nice nipperbat. Ooh." And she got to her feet and toddled out of the kitchen at once.

"Oh no you don't," Oliver told her, following quickly behind. "He's out of bounds to you. Understand?"

"Me *like* nipperbat," the Witch Baby said, scrambling up the stairs at top speed.

"All right, but just looking, okay? Not touching," Oliver said.

Once in Oliver's bedroom, the Witch Baby tottered straight over to Nippy's cage. "Hello, nipperbat," she said, in a friendly voice.

"Hello," Nippy replied, opening one eye and inspecting her.

"Nice nipperbat," the Witch Baby said approvingly. "Good." She gazed at Nippy for a few moments, then turned away. "Me play now. Yes." She heaved herself into Oliver's hammock and swung to and fro, giggling and waving her chubby legs in the air.

Oliver grinned. His baby sister was very cute sometimes. And he was really glad she wasn't that interested in Nippy after all.

He unpacked his Halloween present and Nippy's bat food from his pocket, then looked around. The Witch Baby had her eyes shut and was snoring little yellow bubbles.

"I'll just get you some pond water," Oliver said to Nippy. "Back in two minutes."

Humming to himself, he ran downstairs and out into the backyard where he scooped up a jug of weedy green pond water.

Oh, and there were a few fat slugs squirming over his mom's mold-cabbages. Lovely! Nippy would enjoy them, he thought, gathering them up with a smile. Then he went upstairs again.

The Witch Baby was waving out of Oliver's window when he came back. "Bye bye," she was saying. "Bye bye, nipperbat."

Oliver stopped dead in his tracks. He almost dropped the pond water as he realized that Nippy's cage door was wide open. So was the window. "Wh-what happened?" he gulped. "Where's Nippy?"

The Witch Baby waved again. "Bye bye, Nippy," she said cheerfully. Then she turned to Oliver. "Nippy gone now," she said in a matter-of-fact sort of way.

Oliver felt as if he was in a bad dream. He rushed to the window, spilling pond water everywhere, and leaned out of it. "Nippy! Nippy! Come back!" he yelled.

He could just about see a single
dark speck on the horizon – and then it
grew too small to be seen anymore.

Nippy had gone.

Chapter Three

Oliver couldn't believe it. He simply couldn't believe it. Why had he left his sister alone with Nippy like that? How could he have been so stupid?

The Witch Baby, sensing all was not well, toddled quickly out of the room, and Oliver slumped into his hammock, feeling sick. Mr. Goosepimple was going to be really angry with him for losing Nippy. And the rest of his class would hate him!

Oliver put his head in his hands. Hadn't Mr. Goosepimple said that Nippy hated open spaces? The poor thing was probably terrified to be out on his own. He was sure to get lost or hurt, and he'd be hungry without anyone to feed him. Poor Nippy!

Oliver groaned. What was he going to do?

A coil of blue smoke suddenly drifted under his nose, and Oliver sat bolt upright. Of course! His *Wish In A Box*! The perfect way to get Nippy back. Thank goodness!

Oliver ran over and grabbed the silver

box at once. "I wish I could find Nippy again!" he said loudly.

The box shone an electric blue, and burst open. Clouds of blue smoke rolled out, along with a small sprite, coughing and choking.

"Your wish…cough-cough…has been granted," it spluttered, with a grand bow.

Oliver grinned in relief. "Fantastic. Thank you," he sighed. He kneeled down and peered into Nippy's cage – but it was empty. "So…where is he?" he asked the sprite.

The sprite grinned mischievously. "What, you mean you wanted to find him right now?" he asked. "You should have said!"

Oliver stared at the chuckling sprite. "What do you mean? When *will* I find him, then?" he cried.

The sprite shrugged. "I don't know," he said. "You wished to find him again, and you will. Just…not today. Maybe not tomorrow either. Maybe not all year!"

Oliver's mouth fell open in dismay.

"Wishing in haste leaves a very bad taste," the sprite chanted cheerfully. "Wishing too quick makes you feel quite sick. Wishing in a rush is—"

"All right, all right," Oliver growled. "Don't rub it in."

The sprite poked out his tongue, then vanished with another puff of smoke. Oliver sighed. First he'd lost the school pet, and now he'd wasted his free wish. Why had he ever thought the Halloween break would be fun?

*

"We're looking for a nipperbat," Oliver said to Mr. Periwinkle the next morning. Nippy hadn't returned to the Moons' house, so, after a long, sleepless night, Oliver and his mom had come to Periwinkle's Pet Shop, in the hope that someone might have found Nippy and brought him there.

"A nipperbat? Certainly," Mr. Periwinkle said, pushing his spectacles higher up his nose. "I've got a couple of babies – charming fellows. This way!"

"No, I mean, we've *lost* a nipperbat, and we were wondering if someone had turned him in," Oliver said quickly. He looked down as a skinny black cat wound itself around his legs, then blinked at him with bright green eyes.

"Ahh," Mr. Periwinkle said. "No. Sorry." He shook his head until his whiskers wobbled. "Have you tried the Lost Pet Shelter?"

"Yes," Mrs. Moon replied. "Only a few homeless toads and a stray griffin there."

Oliver explained the whole story to the shopkeeper. "I don't know where else we can look," he finished sadly.

"Unless…" Mrs. Moon brightened. "You know, these nipperbats all look pretty similar to me. We could buy a replacement, couldn't we?"

For the first time all morning, Oliver felt a faint flicker of hope. He knew he was going to get into trouble at school if he didn't bring Nippy back – but perhaps

if he bought a new nipperbat for the class,
Mr. Goosepimple wouldn't be angry.
"Erm...that might help...
I suppose," he said thoughtfully.

"Well, as I said, I do have a couple of
baby nipperbats," Mr. Periwinkle said,
"but they're very small. They can't
speak very well yet."

A red parrot banged
its beak against
a nearby
cage. "Norris!"
it squawked,
with a meaningful
look at Mr. Periwinkle. "Norris!"

"Who's Norris?" Oliver said eagerly.

Mr. Periwinkle hesitated before replying.
"Well, Norris *is* a fully grown nipperbat,

yes," he replied, "but…" He coughed. "He's rather a handful. Something of a character, shall we say."

"That's okay," Oliver replied. He didn't feel he had much choice. He couldn't face going back to school with no nipperbat whatsoever!

"Very well," Mr. Periwinkle said. "Follow me."

The little old wizard led Oliver and his mom farther into the shop. Huge, colorful snakes lay in fat coils on shelves. Wolf cubs practiced their howls in a large pen, while a striped lizard snoozed above them. Piranhas and river sharks snapped at each other in a vast tank of water, and a couple of squabblehawks screeched as they flew around the shop.

"Here he is," Mr. Periwinkle said. "Norris."

Oliver gazed into the cage. Hanging upside down, with his wings folded tightly around himself, was a sleeping black nipperbat. He looked exactly like Nippy. Oliver had to stop himself from whooping and jumping up and down with relief. "Perfect," he breathed. "We'll take him!"

Mr. Periwinkle magicked Norris to the Moons' house with a Transporta spell, and Oliver smiled happily when he got home and saw the new nipperbat safely in Nippy's cage and still fast asleep. Yes! Everything was going to be all right. Everything was going to be absolutely...

Norris opened one
eye. "Oi! Who are
you? And
what kind of
dump is this?"
he squeaked
indignantly,
staring at Oliver.

Oliver gave him a friendly smile.
"Hello," he said. "I'm Oliver, and this is my
bedroom. Next week, I'm going to take you
to my school, which is where you're going
to be living, okay? And then you'll be a
class nipperbat, so you'll need to learn some
potion recipes to help the students, and—"

"Hold on, hold on," Norris interrupted.
He swung himself the right way up and
flew to the side of the cage, where he glared

accusingly at Oliver. "For starters, I ain't learning no recipes. So don't even bother trying! And for seconds—"

"The thing is, though, Nippy – I mean, Norris," Oliver said, "I really need you to—"

Norris ignored him. "The referee's an ogre!" he shouted tunelessly. "The referee's an ogre!"

54

Oliver blinked. "What?" he asked in surprise.

"*He's tall, he's weird, he's got a silver beard, Micky Starr, Micky Starr!*" Norris sang.

Oliver blinked again. "Micky Starr?" he echoed. Micky Starr was the hero of the local Wizardball team, Cacklewick Lightnings.

"Come on, you Lightnings! Come on, you Lightnings!" Norris bellowed. "Get in there, my son! Get in there!"

"Are you a Lightnings fan, then, Norris?" Oliver asked politely.

Norris puffed out his chest with pride. "A fan? I used to belong to Alex Ravenwing, the Lightnings' manager!" he told Oliver. "Until he gave me the sack, that is. Too noisy, he said. Too naughty 'n' all." His black eyes glittered. "So now here I am with you. Your lucky day, ain't it?"

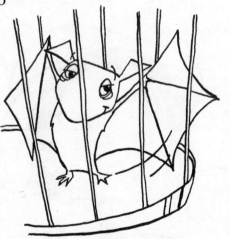

Oliver tried to smile, but he felt like groaning in despair. No, this was not his lucky day. In fact, ever since he'd offered to look after the school nipperbat, he'd had nothing but *bad* luck!

Chapter
Four

Norris made himself at home very
quickly. "I'm not like them other
nipperbats," he told Oliver. "I like to be
out and about. Freedom! That's what I
like. Open this cage door for me, so I can
stretch my wings, there's a good boy."

Oliver hesitated. He really didn't want
to lose two nipperbats in two days. He

double-checked that all the windows in the house were shut, then opened Norris's cage door.

"Whoopee! Here I go!" screeched Norris, whizzing up to the lampshade. *"He's small! A shrimp! I reckon he's a wimp, Ollie Moon! Ollie Moon!"*

"Hey!" Oliver said, stung by Norris's new song. "You can cut that out for a start." He fumbled for his wand. "I'll cast a Silence spell on you if you don't watch it."

"You'll have to catch me first," Norris shouted, zooming out of Oliver's bedroom. His voice came floating up the stairs to Oliver. *"He's short, he's fat, he loves his nipperbat, Ollie Moon! Ollie Moon!"*

"I am not short, or fat, or a wimp," Oliver growled to himself. "And if that bat doesn't watch it, he's going to be lunch."

Oliver stumped downstairs to find Norris tugging at Mr. Moon's new beard, with his sharp little claws.

"Get off me, you pest!" Mr. Moon said, disentangling Norris and shooing him away with a rolled-up newspaper.

"He's mad, he's hairy, his wand looks like a fairy's, Mr. Moon, Mr. Moon," Norris teased, whizzing up to the curtain rail, out of reach.

Mrs. Moon sighed as Norris began nipping at the stitches in the curtains. "Was Nippy like this?" she asked Oliver in a low voice. "Norris does seem very naughty, I must say."

"Nippy was lovely," Oliver said pointedly, with a glare at Norris. "He was really helpful, sweet and polite."

Norris let out a horrible cackle, and Mr. Moon reached for his wand. "Well, until Norris starts behaving like that, he's going to have to stay behind bars," he said grimly, and waved his wand. "Swizzle ka-vat, cage that bat!"

"Hey!" squeaked Norris in protest —
but he'd vanished before he could say
another word.

Mr. Moon sat down thankfully and
shook out his *Cacklewick Chronicle* once
more. "And he can stay there all week —
and definitely while the Wartwhistles are
here," he said. "I'm not having that bat
ruin our dinner party!"

*

Frank and Betty Wartwhistle had been at school with Oliver's parents. They now owned Fiddlesticks Limited, a designer broomstick company, and were worth a small fortune. Every now and then, they invited themselves to dinner with the Moons, which meant days of stress for Oliver's parents as they tried to make the house look presentable for their guests, and agonized about which food to serve. This time, there was even more pressure. The Wartwhistles had let it be known that they were looking for a new sales manager — and that they had their eye on Mr. Moon as a possibility!

Mr. Moon hated his current job, selling ValuStix broomsticks, which were cheaply

made and broke easily. A job at
Fiddlesticks would be a dream come true.

Luckily Oliver's parents were so
wrapped up in the dinner party
preparations, they didn't have time to
pay much attention to Norris over the
next few days. On Monday and Tuesday,
they were so busy decorating the kitchen
with slime-green paint that they didn't
notice that Norris had taught the Witch
Baby some very rude songs.

On Wednesday and Thursday, they were so busy poring over cookbooks that they didn't realize that Norris had managed to get out of his cage and was sampling all the baking.

Then, on Friday night at seven o'clock precisely, the doorbell let out a cackle. *AH-HA-HA-HA-HA-HA!*

"That'll be the Wartwhistles," Mr. Moon said, straightening his pointy hat.

Mrs. Moon gave an anxious sigh. "I'll go and let them in," she said. "Oh, I really hope nothing goes wrong tonight!"

Chapter Five

"Happy Halloween! Come on in," Oliver heard his mom saying. She led the Wartwhistles into the living room, where the rest of the family were. "Frank, Betty, what can I get you to drink?"

"Slug champagne would hit the spot," Mrs. Wartwhistle said with her nose in the air.

Mrs. Moon's smile faded. "Oh. We don't actually have any slug champagne, but we do have a lovely eel wine I could pour you, or…"

Mrs. Wartwhistle wrinkled her nose in distaste. "I *told* you we should have brought some champagne with us," she said to her husband in a loud whisper. "I *told* you the Moons couldn't afford champagne!"

Oliver could see his mom and dad were embarrassed by her comments. "I could magic up a fizzy potion for you instead," he suggested. "And we've got fresh slugs I could pop into it, if you like."

Mr. Wartwhistle looked as if he'd rather wrestle with a crocodile. "Charming…but no," he said, with a shudder. "Plain nettle juice will be fine."

"Nettle juice for me, too," Mrs. Wartwhistle sighed. She sat down heavily in an armchair. "Next time we come, we'll bring champagne," she said. "We forgot you were too poor to buy your own."

Mr. Moon clamped his lips tight together as if he was worried he might say something rude.

"Nettle juice it is," Mrs. Moon managed to say brightly. "Coming right up!"

Just then, Oliver heard a familiar voice coming from upstairs. *"He's rude, he's big, he needs to get a wig, Frankie Wart, Frankie Wart…"*

Oh, no! Norris sounded extra loud tonight. Oliver coughed hastily, hoping the Wartwhistles hadn't heard the naughty nipperbat, and went to close the living room door. But to his horror, there came Norris swooping down the stairs... and straight into the room!

"Evenin' all!" Norris said chirpily, flying up to perch on the mantelpiece. He winked at Oliver. "You really should check the catch on that cage door, son. It's not hard for a clever bat like me to undo it, you know. Not hard at all!"

Mr. Moon reached for his wand. "I think you'd better go back upstairs, Norris," he warned.

"Not likely," Norris said, dodging up the chimney. *"She's rude, and snobby, her nose is very blobby, Betty Wart, Betty Wart..."*

"I've never been so insulted!" Mrs.
Wartwhistle hissed, glaring at the
chimney with narrow yellow eyes.
"Frank! Are you going to sit there and let
that thing call us names?"

"I certainly am not! Come out, you
'orrible creature!" cried Mr. Wartwhistle,
striding over to the chimney and poking
his head up it.

Seconds later, he withdrew his head, wiping his eye. "Nasty little thing just kicked soot at me. Really! I don't think I want to stay here another minute!"

"Bye bye," the Witch Baby chirruped sweetly. "Bye bye, Warts."

"I'm very sorry," Mr. Moon said, wringing his hands. "As soon as that bat comes out, I'll get rid of it and we can enjoy our Halloween dinner. We've spent hours cooking for you. We've made a special—"

"I don't think so," Mrs. Wartwhistle said frostily. She got to her feet. "Come on, Frank. We're going."

Mrs. Moon came back into the room just as the front door slammed shut behind the departing Wartwhistles. She was carrying a jug of nettle juice and some goblets on a tray, and she looked confused. "Everything all right?" she asked.

"Not really," Mr. Moon said, through clenched teeth. "There goes my chance of a job at Fiddlesticks."

"*Me* good," the Witch Baby beamed, then pointed to the chimney. "Norris bad."

"Couldn't have put it better myself," Mr. Moon said. "That nipperbat is a complete nightmare!"

It was true, Oliver thought on Monday morning, as he walked into the classroom with all the other students. Norris *was* a nightmare. He had ruined the Halloween break. If only Nippy hadn't flown away like that on the first day!

Oliver heaved Norris's cage onto the table beside Mr. Goosepimple's desk. He'd carried the cage to school himself, rather than risk sending it with a spell and have Norris get up to any mischief before Oliver had even arrived. "This is the classroom, Norris," he said in a whisper. "Please try to be quiet. Try to

be nice. I'm sure you can do it!" In truth, he wasn't sure of any such thing, but he was desperate.

Mr. Goosepimple looked at Norris, then at Oliver, with a strange expression on his face. "Did everything go all right, Oliver?" he asked.

Oliver took a deep breath. Time to own up to what had happened. He knew already that the whole class was going to hate him for it! "Well... not exactly, sir," he muttered. "You see..."

Norris chose that moment to let out

a huge belch, then blow a raspberry,
which made some of the
young wizards and
witches giggle.

"Manners, Nippy!"
called out Pippi
Prowlcat in surprise.

"Go on, Oliver," Mr.
Goosepimple urged, leaning closer.
"What were you going to say?"

Oliver could feel his neck grow hot.
He had been dreading this moment all
week – confessing that he'd lost Nippy.
Mr. Goosepimple was going to be
soooo angry. He was sure to send Oliver
to Mrs. MacLizard for a truly awful
punishment!

Oliver cleared his throat. "Well…I'm

afraid that…" He coughed. "I'm really sorry to say that—"

"Go on, just tell 'em," Norris said loudly. "You lost Nippy. And now you're trying to trick 'em with me instead!" And with that, he gave a great cackle of laughter that made the windows rattle.

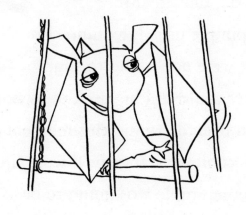

Chapter
Six

A deathly hush fell upon the classroom.
Oliver could feel everyone's eyes burning
into him.

"You *lost* Nippy?" Hattie Toadtrumper
cried indignantly. "You *lost* him?"

Oliver glared at Norris, and then
turned to face the class. "Yes," he
mumbled. "And I'm really, really sorry,

everyone, but you see—"

"Poor Nippy!" sobbed Hattie.

"I knew it should have been me looking after Nippy!" Lucy Lizardlegs said, shooting a fierce look at Oliver. "*I* would have taken more care of him!"

Oliver didn't know where to look. This was even worse than he'd feared!

"Settle down, settle down!" Mr. Goosepimple ordered, tapping his wand on his desk for silence. "There is actually a happy ending to this story."

Oliver blinked. "There is?" he asked doubtfully.

Mr. Goosepimple nodded. "Mr. Bogscraper, the caretaker, said he found Nippy huddled in the school porch on the very first morning of the school break! And he's down here, look!" Mr. Goosepimple bent down and pulled something out from under his desk. It was a different bat cage – with Nippy inside it!

A cheer went up from the class,
and then, with a puff of blue smoke,
the smirking sprite
from Oliver's
Wish In A Box
reappeared.
"Didn't I tell
you you'd find
him again?"
he said to Oliver
mischievously, before vanishing once more.

Oliver stared at Nippy in astonishment.
"Oh, Nippy, I'm so glad you're all right!"
he cried joyfully. "I'm really sorry I left
you alone with my sister! I've been
worrying about you all week."

Nippy gave him a little smile. "No
harm done," he said shyly.

Oliver grinned, then pointed his wand at Norris's cage. "I can send Norris straight back to the pet shop if you like, sir," he suggested. Norris had caused so much trouble, Oliver was looking forward to seeing the back of him!

Norris was staring out of the classroom window watching intently as Ms. Smokeweaver refereed some of the older students in a Wizardball match. "Go on, my son – shoot!" Norris called out excitedly. "And he scores! Two-nil to the purples!"

Mr. Goosepimple gazed thoughtfully at Norris. "Let's not do anything hasty," Mr. Goosepimple said to Oliver, stroking his beard. "I'll speak to Mrs. MacLizard first."

To Oliver's huge relief, Norris was dispatched to Mrs. MacLizard's office with a messenger sprite a few minutes later, and lessons began. All right, so there was a Potions quiz to slog through, and an hour of Toad Training, but then it was their Monday Wizardball practice, which was always fun.

Once Oliver and his friends had changed and were out on the field, Oliver saw to his great surprise that Mrs. MacLizard was watching from the sidelines – with Norris perched on her shoulder.

Norris seemed to be enjoying himself very much. *"He's fast, he's bold, he scores a smashing goal, Jakey-boy, Jakey-boy!"* he cheered, as Jake shot the ball through the hoop.

"*She's smart, she's quick, she gives the ball a flick, Hattie T, Hattie T!*" he sang, as Hattie Toadtrumper flicked in a second goal.

Then Oliver had the ball. He bounced it the length of the field, feeling Norris's beady eyes upon him. He passed one player, then another…then he jumped up and scored! Oliver braced himself for a rude song from Norris. Surely the nipperbat couldn't keep up his niceness for long?

*"He's hot, he's cool,
the greatest kid in
school, Ollie
Moon! Ollie
Moon!"* sang
Norris, with
a wink.

Oliver laughed
and did a thumbs up at him. "Thanks,
Norris," he said. "You're not so bad
yourself."

At the end of the match, Mrs.
MacLizard waved her wand and
magically summoned the entire school
to the Wizardball pitch. "I have a very
exciting announcement to make," she
said. "I know you were all upset about
Hoo-Hoo's retirement, but I think I've

found a replacement. Norris, we'd love you to be our new Wizardball mascot and have a home here at Magic School…as long as you promise not to sing anything *too* rude about the opposition. What do you say?"

Norris flew around her head in excitement, then perched back on her shoulder, his eyes bright. He stared out at the students and cleared his throat.

"I like you mob,
I'll say yes to your job,
Magic School, Magic School.
I'm pleased! I'm proud,
To sing my songs out loud,
Magic School!
Magic School!"

Everyone cheered, then Norris gave Oliver another wink. "Sorry if I was a difficult house guest, Oliver," he said, rather sheepishly. "I've just missed my Wizardball, that's all. No offense, mate."

"None taken," Oliver laughed. "Welcome to Magic School, Norris!"

Don't miss Oliver's fab website,
where you can find lots of fun, free stuff.
Log on now...

www.olivermoon.com